Winter
Is Coming

Tony Johnston   Illustrated by Jim LaMarche

A Paula Wiseman Book
Simon & Schuster Books for Young Readers
New York London Toronto Sydney New Delhi

For Florence and Wendell Minor, two people full of light
—T. J.

For Lee Bernd, whose love of children's literature
was a gift to all her students
—J. L.

SIMON & SCHUSTER BOOKS FOR YOUNG READERS
An imprint of Simon & Schuster Children's Publishing Division
1230 Avenue of the Americas, New York, New York 10020
Text copyright © 2014 by Susan T. Johnston and Roger D. Johnston, Trustees of the Johnston Family Trust
Illustrations copyright © 2014 by Jim LaMarche
All rights reserved, including the right of reproduction in whole or in part in any form.
SIMON & SCHUSTER BOOKS FOR YOUNG READERS is a trademark of Simon & Schuster, Inc.
For information about special discounts for bulk purchases, please contact Simon & Schuster Special Sales at
1-866-506-1949 or business@simonandschuster.com.
The Simon & Schuster Speakers Bureau can bring authors to your live event. For more information or to
book an event, contact the Simon & Schuster Speakers Bureau at 1-866-248-3049 or visit our website at
www.simonspeakers.com.
Book design by Lizzy Bromley
The text for this book is set in Adobe Garamond.
The illustrations for this book are rendered in acrylics, colored pencils, and
opaque inks on Arches watercolor paper.
Manufactured in the United States of America
0115 PCR
10 9 8 7 6 5 4 3 2
Library of Congress Cataloging-in-Publication Data
Johnston, Tony.
Winter is coming / Tony Johnston ; illustrated by Jim LaMarche. — 1st ed.
p. cm.
"A Paula Wiseman Book."
Summary: Each day, from September through November, brings glimpses of forest animals seeking food in
preparation for the onset of winter, from a fox sniffing the last apple on the ground to a flock of wild turkeys
that finds nothing.
ISBN 978-1-4424-7251-8 (hard cover : alk. paper)
1. Forest animals—Juvenile fiction. [1. Forest animals—Fiction. 2. Autumn—Fiction.] I. LaMarche, Jim, ill.
II. Title.
PZ10.3.J715Win 2014
[E]—dc23
2012040457
ISBN 978-1-4424-7253-2 (eBook)

It is a cold September day.
Fall is still here but ice
is in the air. I feel it.
Winter is coming.

A red fox slips into the clearing
that I am watching.
First-sun hits its back.
The red fox shines like a small red
fire.
I am quiet, quiet.
The red fox is quiet, quiet.
We share this place.

The red fox sniffs the last apple
on our apple tree. The apple is wrinkled
like my grandma's face.
But, wrinkled or not, it is food.
And winter is coming.

Today a mother bear and her cub
rustle through the trees.
I do not rustle.
I hold my breath
so they will stay.
The mother bear snuffles for food
among the flaming leaves. The cub
snuffles too. But no luck.
They go away
searching, searching.
Winter is coming.

Now it's October.
A family of skunks waddles
along the fringe of the woods.
Skunks love night most, but sometimes
they roam in daytime.
I can smell them before I see them.
Not a bad smell; a real smell.
My father says
animals are true
to themselves.
Skunks are skunks.
They sniff where the wrinkled apple
was. The one the red fox took.
The skunks must look harder
for something to eat.
Winter is coming.

This morning I'm up at dawn.
I see a pair of woodpeckers, red heads
hammering. They riddle
a big tree with holes.
Then they plug the holes
with acorns they found somewhere.
Whatever they can scrounge.
Whatever other animals
have not found.
Animals do not waste.
The woodpeckers keep hammering.
Winter is coming
fast.

On this day rabbits come, bringing quiet
with them.
Their noses quiver, testing the air
for food—
and danger. Danger is everywhere.
I know animals don't harm
on purpose.
They harm only for food,
or to save themselves
or their babies.
The rabbits find some skinny
weeds and begin gnawing.
They are lucky—for now. But
winter is coming.

October is gone.
Moon rises early.
A ways off, a lynx ghosts along,
all shining.
A lynx with black-tipped
ears. A lynx with Egypt
eyes. A lynx the color
of moon.
My mother says wild things
are full of light. I believe that.
I stay quiet, quiet
to keep it here—
for a moment.
It paws out a beetle
from the frozen leaves.
The lynx is hungry,
so it eats the beetle.
Winter is coming.

November afternoon. Two stripy
chipmunks ripple
from branch to branch
of a pine. Looking
and chattering. Chattering
and looking. They find
pinecones. They hold them
in their little paws
and chew at them
and gobble the seeds
and stuff their cheeks
and spit out the husks.
The busy chipmunks
are beautiful, I think,
gobbling as fast as they can.
Winter is coming.

On this day a mother deer
comes walking carefully.
A doe with two fawns.
The fawns blend into the shadows.
The deer nibble the needles
of spruce. They nibble
the brittle grass. They nibble
at the edges of ferns. They nibble
at nothing. Once the doe
comes so close I could touch her.
But I don't. I know that animals
are best left alone.
Maybe the deer will find enough food.
Maybe not.
Soon they move on, nibbling.
Winter is coming.

Another day.
And oh! Canada geese, honkers,
pass high above. They are flying
in a wide gray V, looking for
a warmer place.
Each year they do that. Something
tells them when to leave.
Who knows what?
I love honkers.
I love their song.
Gray. And sad. And old.
I watch them for a long time.
Winter is coming.
The honkers know.
And they go.

Today no animals come.
Not one.
The clearing and the trees are filled with
silence.
And wildness.
And cold.
They are waiting for something.
Winter is coming.

Dawn burns the sky.
A flock of wild turkeys jostles by.
They poke everyplace, muttering
food, food, food.
We can learn from animals, my father says.
About patience. About truth. About quiet.
About taking only what you need
from the land because
we are just its keepers.
I pay attention to the wild turkeys.
Suddenly the wild turkeys flurry away
without warning.
Winter is coming.

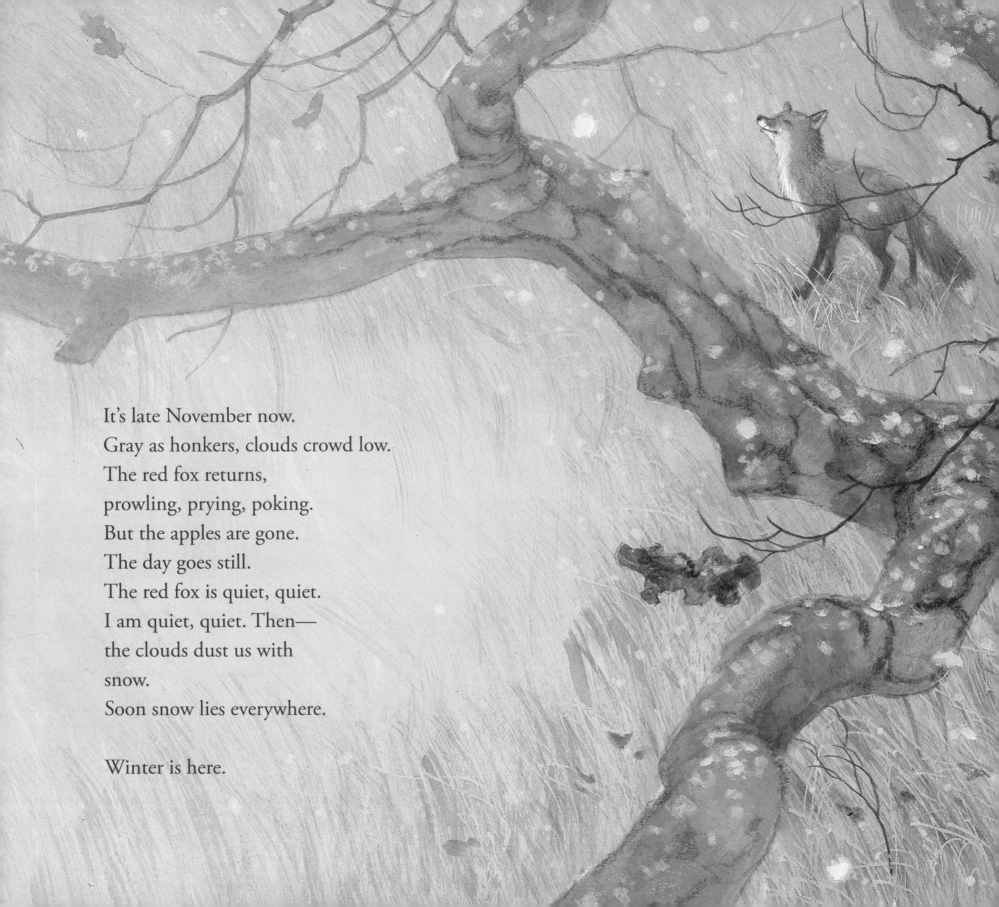

It's late November now.
Gray as honkers, clouds crowd low.
The red fox returns,
prowling, prying, poking.
But the apples are gone.
The day goes still.
The red fox is quiet, quiet.
I am quiet, quiet. Then—
the clouds dust us with
snow.
Soon snow lies everywhere.

Winter is here.

Chipmunk

Red Fox

Wild Turkey

Lynx

Rabbit